# I Hate Rules!

For Trina—N.K.
For Babette—J&W

ISBN 0-439-80092-7

12 11 10 9 8 7 6                                        8 9 10/0

Printed in the U.S.A.                        40

First Scholastic printing, September 2005

# I Hate Rules!

by Nancy Krulik • illustrated by John & Wendy

SCHOLASTIC INC.
New York Toronto London Auckland Sydney
Mexico City New Delhi Hong Kong Buenos Aires

# Chapter 1

"Ouch!"

Katie Carew groaned when George Brennan tagged her. George was a lot bigger than Katie. Sometimes he tagged too hard.

"Gotcha, Katie Kazoo!" George shouted, using the special nickname he'd given her. "Now you're part of the chain."

Katie frowned. She was always the first one tagged when they played Train Tag. Katie wasn't a very fast runner.

But she wasn't a bad sport, either. She linked her arm through George's without complaining. Together, they ran after Miriam Chan.

"You're tagged!" George cheered as he bashed into Miriam's side.

Miriam rubbed her arm where George had tagged her. "How come you guys never go after Jeremy or Kevin?"

"Because they're too fast," George explained. "Join the train."

Miriam slipped her arm through Katie's. "Now who should we try to tag?" she asked.

George looked around the playground. Jeremy Fox was there. So was Mandy Banks. They were both really fast. George couldn't catch them on his own—never mind when he was running with Miriam and Katie.

Then Suzanne Lock strolled onto the playground. She was wearing cowboy boots and a skirt. That wasn't a great outfit for running. She'd be an easy catch. "Let's get Suzanne!" George answered.

George took off in Suzanne's direction. He pulled Katie and Miriam behind him.

"Gotcha!" Miriam and George cried out as

they reached Suzanne.

"Join the train," Katie added.

"No, thank you," Suzanne answered.

"What do you mean, 'No thank you'?" George demanded to know. "We tagged you, so you have to join the train."

"No I don't," Suzanne told him. "Train Tag is for kids."

"We *are* kids," George reminded her.

"Well, I've got more grown-up things to do." Suzanne reached into her pocket and pulled out a cell phone. "I have to make a call."

"Hey! Whose is that?" Miriam asked.

"Mine," Suzanne answered.

Katie had seen that phone before. It really belonged to Suzanne's dad. But Katie didn't say anything. She didn't want to embarrass her best friend.

"How come you brought your cell phone to school?" Miriam asked.

"You never know when you might need to

call someone," Suzanne told her.

"Hey, Katie Kazoo. You know what you get when you mix a telephone with a pair of scissors?" George asked.

"What?" Katie asked.

"Snippy answers!"

Katie giggled. She loved when George told jokes.

Suzanne didn't. Instead of laughing, she pulled a headset from her backpack. "I can talk on the phone and still use my hands," Suzanne explained. She plugged the headset into the phone.

"My mom has one of those in her office," Miriam told her. "You look really grown up, Suzanne."

Suzanne smiled.

Just then, Katie's other best friend, Jeremy Fox, came running over. "Hey! Mrs. Derkman is going to make us line up any minute. We don't have much time left to play. Come on!"

"You guys go ahead," Suzanne said. "I'll

just stay here with my phone."

But before the kids could go back to their game, Mrs. Derkman blew her whistle. "Class 3A," the teacher called out, "let's line up."

"Boy, that math homework was really hard," Katie whispered to Jeremy as they got in line.

"It took a long time," Jeremy agreed.

George looked at them both strangely.

"Math homework? We had math homework?"

"You didn't do it?" Katie asked.

George turned red in the face. "I . . . uh . . . I guess I forgot."

"Oh man," Jeremy moaned. "This stinks."

"Why?" Katie asked him. "*George* forgot his homework. Not you."

"I know," Jeremy agreed. "But George, you were supposed to be in the four-square championship at recess. You're the best four-square player in our whole class."

George smiled. "I'm the king. I'm going to destroy the kids in 3B."

Jeremy shook his head. "No you're not. You're not even going to be there. You know the rule. If you forget your homework, you have to do it at recess."

George didn't look so happy anymore. "Mrs. Derkman has too many rules," he moaned as he got into line.

# Chapter 2

Katie walked into the classroom and hung her jacket on the third hook from the left.

Then she placed her homework in the bin on Mrs. Derkman's desk.

Finally, she sat down at her desk and began to copy the spelling words on the board.

Katie did the same thing every morning. Mrs. Derkman had very strict rules about how you behaved in her classroom.

George sniffed at the air as he put away his coat. "*Ooh*. Do you have tuna fish again, Manny? Or did you just forget to shower?"

A few kids chuckled. Mrs. Derkman did

not. "If you have a question, George, please raise your hand," she said.

George sat down quietly and pulled out his notebook.

Just then a small piece of paper landed on Katie's desk. It was a note from Suzanne. Katie read the note and scribbled an answer.

"Kevin, pass this to Suzanne?" Katie whispered as she folded the paper. Kevin sat between Katie and Suzanne.

"No way," he whispered back. "I'm not getting in trouble."

Katie frowned, but she understood. Mrs. Derkman didn't like kids passing notes in class. It wasn't Kevin's note. Why should he risk it?

Katie waited until Mrs. Derkman was looking the other way. Then she tossed the note to Suzanne.

Katie almost hoped Suzanne *wouldn't* write back. If Mrs. Derkman caught the girls writing notes, she was sure to do something

mean. Something absolutely horrible.
Something . . .

"Suzanne, give me that note," Mrs.
Derkman ordered.

Oh no! Mrs. Derkman had seen them.

Suzanne looked at Katie and bit her lip.
She didn't move. It looked like she was frozen.

"Suzanne, you heard me." Mrs. Derkman

held out her hand.

Suzanne stood up. She walked slowly toward the front of the room. All the kids were staring. All except Katie. She couldn't even look at her.

"Thank you," Mrs. Derkman said when Suzanne handed her the note. "Please go back to your seat."

Katie breathed a sigh of relief. That wasn't so bad.

But Mrs. Derkman wasn't finished. She opened the note and began to read it . . . *out loud!*

"My mother bought me these horrible pink flowery underpants. They're for babies." Mrs. Derkman read Suzanne's words.

Suzanne buried her

head in her arms.

"Do you have to wear them?" Mrs. Derkman continued, reading Katie's part of the note.

"I'm wearing them right now." Mrs. Derkman said, as she read what Suzanne had just written.

The teacher looked at Suzanne and Katie. "I don't think that was so important that it couldn't wait until lunch. Do you girls?"

At first no one in the class said anything.

Then, a few of the boys started to giggle.
Soon, everyone was laughing really hard.

"Pink flower underpants," Manny
Gonzalez howled. "Real stylin', Suzanne!"

"I see England, I see France, I see
Suzanne's flower underpants," George began
to chant.

Suzanne looked like she was about to cry.
"I wish I could hide under a big rock," she
moaned quietly.

Katie looked up at the ceiling. What if a
giant rock really did come falling down?
What if it landed right on Suzanne's head?

But no rock fell from the sky. In fact,
nothing happened at all. Katie breathed a
sigh of relief. Suzanne had been lucky. Her
wish hadn't come true.

Katie knew all about wishes that came
true. She knew you had to be careful what
you wished for. Not all wishes turned out
great.

It had all started one really bad day. Katie

had ruined her favorite jeans and burped in front of the whole class. Katie had wished that she could be anyone but herself.

There must have been a shooting star flying overhead or something when Katie made her wish because the very next day, a magic wind blew. It was like a tornado that stormed just around Katie. The wind turned Katie into Speedy, the class hamster! That had been awful. Katie had been completely naked— except for Speedy's fur, of course.

Luckily, Katie had changed back into herself before anyone realized who was really chomping on Speedy's chew sticks. *Un*luckily, the magic wind returned. That time it turned Katie into Lucille, the school's lunch lady. She'd had to serve the kids gloppy egg salad and old milk. *Blech!*

Even that wasn't as bad as the time the magic wind turned Katie into Suzanne's baby sister, Heather. Eating cafeteria food tasted good compared to sucking smelly baby formula from a bottle.

The weirdest thing the magic wind ever did was turn Katie into Jeremy Fox. That had been a real mess. Katie hadn't known whether to go to the boys' room or the girls' room. Even worse, she'd almost lost Jeremy as a friend.

The magic wind hadn't been back for a while. But Katie had a feeling it wasn't through with her yet. She couldn't be sure when the wind would come, or who it would turn her into next.

That's why Katie didn't make wishes anymore. You never knew what could happen if they came true.

# Chapter 3

Miriam Chan sat down at the cafeteria table beside her best friend, Mandy Banks. "Come on, let's do 'I Wanna Send a Letter,'" she said before she even unpacked her lunch.

Mandy swallowed a bite of her egg salad sandwich and nodded. Then the two girls stood up and began playing a new clapping game.

*"Mail a letter to a boy from camp, camp, camp.*
*Seal the envelope with a stamp, stamp, stamp.*
*He's the one I always miss, miss, miss,*
*So I seal it with a kiss, kiss, kiss.*
*Hope he gets it in a snap, snap, snap,*
*And sends a note to make me clap, clap, clap."*
Everyone watched as Miriam and Mandy

played their new game. The girls stamped
their feet when they said 'stamp,' missed when
they said 'miss,' blew kisses, snapped their fingers, and clapped their hands.

"Hey, can you teach me that?" Katie asked
when the girls finished.

"Sure. I'll show you after lunch," Mandy
agreed.

"Me too?" Zoe Canter asked.

"Of course," Miriam said. "We can do it while we watch the four-square championship."

"I think my mother used to play a game like that," Suzanne told the others. She reached into her pocket and pulled out her cell phone. " I'll call her and find out."

But before Suzanne could dial her mother, George grabbed the phone from her hands. He raced to the other side of the table and began to push numbers on the phone.

"Who are you calling?" Suzanne cried.

"It doesn't matter," George replied. "I'm just calling anyone."

"It better not be long distance," Suzanne told him.

George ignored her. "Hello," he said to the person who answered the phone. "Is your refrigerator running?" When the person on the other end said yes, George started giggling. "Then you'd better catch it!" he exclaimed.

George tossed the phone to Katie.

"You've got to hear this, Katie Kazoo!" he shouted.

Katie reached up and caught the phone. She could hear the woman screaming on the other end. "You shouldn't make phony phone calls," Katie told George.

"Especially on *my* phone," Suzanne added.

Just then, Mr. Kane, the principal, walked over to their table. "What have you got there, Katie?" he demanded.

Katie gulped. He sounded really mad. "It's a phone," she said quietly.

"I can see that," Mr. Kane said. "It's against the rules for students to bring cell phones to school."

"This isn't . . ." Katie was about to say that the phone wasn't hers. Then she looked at Suzanne. She seemed like she was about to cry. Katie just couldn't tell Mr. Kane that the phone belonged to Suzanne. Suzanne had had a bad enough day—with her flower underpants and all.

Mr. Kane took the phone from Katie's hands. "You'll get this back at the end of the day."

"Yes sir," Katie said quietly. She turned to sit back in her seat.

But Mr. Kane wasn't finished. "You broke the rules, Katie," he continued. "You'll have to miss recess today. You can spend the time thinking about why we have rules in school."

Mr. Kane walked away. Katie could feel her face getting redder and redder. Everyone was staring at her.

And it wasn't even her fault.

The worst part was now she wouldn't get to learn Mandy and Miriam's clapping game. Everyone would know it but her.

*"I hate rules!"* Katie declared angrily.

# Chapter 4

Katie sat at the empty cafeteria table and looked toward the window. The sun was shining brightly. She could hear the other kids playing outside. They sounded like they were having a lot of fun.

The weather was so nice that Mrs. Derkman had gone to sit on the steps just outside the cafeteria door. That way, she could be outside and still make sure George and Katie didn't get out of their punishment.

Katie took a big, angry bite from a carrot stick. This whole thing was so unfair!

"Hey, Katie Kazoo, how come you can't eat carrots with fingers?" George shouted. He was sitting at a table all the way on the other side of the room.

"Why?" Katie answered.

"Because carrots don't *have* fingers!" George laughed hard at his own joke.

Katie didn't laugh at all. She was too mad. This was all George's fault. "Which end of a carrot is the left end?" George tried another joke.

"I don't know."

George smiled. "The end you don't eat!"

Katie scowled.

"Come on! That one was funny," George said.

Katie shook her head. There was no way she was going to laugh at any of George's jokes today. "Aren't you supposed to be doing math?" she asked before he could tell her another one.

"Oh yeah," George replied. He looked around the table. "I guess I forgot my math book."

Katie couldn't believe it. "You'd better get that book. Mrs. Derkman will really be mad if you don't do the homework," Katie warned.

George couldn't argue with that. "I'll be right back!" Quickly he dashed out of the cafeteria and ran toward room 3A.

Now Katie was all alone. She looked up at the clock on the wall. There were still fifteen minutes of recess to go.

Just then, Katie felt a warm breeze nip at the back of her neck. *Uh-oh!* Mrs. Derkman must be coming back inside. She was going to be really mad that George had left.

Katie turned quickly toward the door. Mrs. Derkman wasn't there. In fact, the door was closed. But the wind was still blowing on the back of Katie's neck. And it wasn't blowing anywhere else in the room.

Katie gulped. She knew what that meant. This was no ordinary wind. This was the magic wind!

The magic wind began spinning faster and faster all around Katie. Her red hair whipped wildly around her head. She shut her eyes tightly, and tried not to cry. As the fierce tornado swirled, she held on to the table and struggled to keep her feet on the floor.

And then it stopped. Just like that. No warning. But Katie wasn't surprised. The magic wind *never* gave any warning. It didn't follow any rules.

Katie was glad that the tornado was over. But she was also very afraid. After all, whenever the wind stopped blowing, Katie turned into someone else.

Slowly, Katie opened her eyes and looked around. Right across from her was the huge mural she and her friends had painted on the cafeteria wall. It was a picture of unicorns riding skateboards over a rainbow.

Okay, so now she knew where she was. But she still didn't know *who* she was.

Katie looked at the tables and chairs in the cafeteria. They suddenly seemed small to her. She glanced down at her hands. They were really big . . . and kind of hairy! Yuck! the nails were all chewed down.

*Who was she?*

Before Katie could figure it out, George came racing back into the cafeteria. "Hey, Katie Kazoo . . . he began. Then he looked around, surprised. He didn't see his friend anywhere.

"Hi, Mr. Kane," he said. "Where did Katie go?"

# Chapter 5

Mr. Kane? Was it possible? Had the magic wind actually turned Katie into the school principal?

Katie looked down. Instead of her T-shirt with the heart on it, she was wearing a white shirt and a navy blue striped tie. Her skirt was gone, too. A pair of gray wool slacks was in its place.

Katie reached up and touched her head. There was a big bald spot where her hair used to be. And when she opened her mouth to speak, a man's deep voice came out. "Katie? I . . . um . . . well . . . I don't know where she is," she told George.

"You mean she skipped out on her punishment?" George sounded impressed.

"I'd better go find her," Katie said quickly. She ran out of the cafeteria and into the hall.

The hallway was very noisy. The kids were coming back inside from recess.

"Hey, Mr. Kane," a fifth-grader named Sam greeted her.

"Hello," Katie said in her deep voice.

"Excuse me, Mr. Kane." Ms. Lobel, a kindergarten teacher, stopped Katie. "Do we still have that faculty meeting after school?"

Katie didn't know what to say. She didn't know anything about faculty meetings. "I . . . uh . . . I'll have to check," she said quickly.

Before she could take another step, Mr. Bloom, a second-grade teacher, came up to her. "Mr. Kane, were you able to look at my supply request form yet?"

"Supply request form?" Katie asked him. She'd never heard of one of those.

Mr. Bloom looked upset. "I really need

those extra notebooks," he said.

"I guess you should get them, then," Katie told him nervously.

"You have to sign the form," Mr. Bloom reminded her. "I'll come by for it later."

Katie knew she had to get out of the hallway before she bumped into anyone else. Everyone thought she was Mr. Kane. They expected her to act like a real principal. But Katie had absolutely no idea what a real principal did.

Katie needed a place to hide until the magic wind came and turned her back into herself. But where could she go?

Just then, Mrs. Davidson, the school secretary, poked her head out of the office. "Mr. Kane," she said, "I left your messages on your desk."

That was it! Katie could hide out in Mr. Kane's office. After all, she *was* the principal.

"Um, thank you," Katie said, trying to sound very principal-like. "I'll get them now."

She dashed into Mr. Kane's office and shut the door.

Katie sat down behind Mr. Kane's big wooden desk and breathed a sigh of relief. At least no one could get to her in here.

She looked around the office. There were crowded bookshelves and stacks of paper everywhere. It looked kind of like Katie's dad's office, except Mr. Kane had wind-up toys on the windowsill, and there was a glass jar filled with chocolates on his desk.

Katie took one of the candies and popped it in her mouth. She leaned back in Mr. Kane's big leather chair and let the chocolate melt on her tongue. This wasn't so bad. She had plenty of snacks to eat, and toys to play with. As long as she stayed in Mr. Kane's office, she couldn't get into any trouble.

Well, that wasn't exactly true. Katie was actually going to be in *a lot* of trouble—as soon as Mrs. Derkman noticed that she wasn't in class. Katie didn't know what the punishment was for that, but she bet it was pretty bad. She *was* breaking a really big rule.

Now Katie was really worried. What if Mrs. Derkman called her mother? What if she called the police? How would Katie ever be able to explain what had happened to her?

Just then, Katie heard Mrs. Davidson's voice come over the loudspeaker. "All students should be in class now."

That gave Katie a great idea. She knew how to make sure she wasn't breaking any rules. Quickly, she leaped up from the chair and ran to the outer office.

"I need to say something," Katie told Mrs. Davidson as she grabbed for the microphone.

"This is Mr. Kane," Katie announced. "From now on, there is one rule in Cherrydale Elementary School. And that rule is . . . *there are no rules!*"

# Chapter 6

At first, the whole school was completely silent. It was as if no one could believe what they had just heard. Then, suddenly, the classroom doors burst open. Kids raced into the halls.

"We're free!" a small girl with pigtails screamed out.

"Last one on the playground is a rotten egg!" yelled a tall, skinny second-grader.

"No rules, rules! No rules, rules! No rules, rules!" a group of fourth-graders chanted as they ran down the hall.

As Katie peeked out of the school office, a crowd of fifth-grade girls spotted her. "Wow.

It's Mr. Kane!" they squealed. "Thank you! Thank you!"

The students were treating Katie like some sort of rock star. As she strolled down the halls of the school, kids of all ages high-fived her. Some ran over to hug her. Katie smiled proudly. She was a hero.

Well, at least the *kids* thought she was a hero. The teachers had a different idea.

"Class 3A, come back here right now!" Mrs. Derkman shouted as her students streamed into the hallway. "It's not recess!"

But the kids didn't come back. Why should they? There was no rule that said they had to be in class.

"Mr. Kane!" Mrs. Derkman called out.

At first Katie jumped. Mrs. Derkman's angry voice scared her. Then Katie remembered. *She* was the principal. That made her Mrs. Derkman's boss.

Katie liked that idea a lot.

"Yes, Mrs. Derkman?" Katie answered. She

tried to sound very official.

"What's going on here?" Mrs. Derkman asked. "My class is going crazy."

"Relax," Katie told the teacher. "They're just having fun."

Before Mrs. Derkman could answer, a huge group of sixth-graders came running by at top speed. They were going so fast, they didn't even see Mrs. Derkman standing in their path. *Whoosh*. The teacher was swept away with the crowd.

"We'll talk about this later, Mr. Kane," Mrs. Derkman shouted as the sixth-grade mob pushed her down the hall.

Katie chuckled as she walked into the cafeteria. She peeked her head into the room. George was still the only kid there. But he wasn't struggling with math homework anymore. He was eating chocolate cake. Lots of chocolate cake.

Usually kids were only allowed one dessert with lunch. Right now, George had at least

ten pieces in front of him. And lunchtime had been over a long time ago.

"Looks like you're having fun," Katie said to George.

"*Mmmph. Phllmph.*" George mumbled through a mouthful of cake. Every time he opened his mouth, more wet, half-eaten chocolate crumbs poured out.

Watching George talk and chew was really gross. "Don't speak, George," Katie told him. "Just eat."

George gave her a big, chocolatey smile, then dove into his next slice of cake.

Suddenly, a whole group of kids came racing into the cafeteria. Jeremy was at the front of the crowd. He held a soccer ball in his hands.

"Where are you all going?" Katie asked them.

"To the yard, Mr. Kane," Jeremy explained with a huge smile. "We're going to play soccer all afternoon."

"Have fun!" Katie told him. She was glad she could make her best friend so happy.

Just then Katie heard laughing—and crying—coming from the computer lab across the hall. She raced to see what was happening.

Inside the lab, Suzanne, Mandy, Zoe, and Miriam were all staring at a picture on one of the computer screens. Suzanne, Mandy, and Miriam were smiling. Zoe was crying.

"What's wrong, Zoe?" Katie asked.

"Oh, don't worry about her, Mr. Kane,"

Suzanne said. "She always gets that way when she thinks about the Bayside Boys."

"We're looking at their official website," Mandy explained. "They just added a bunch of new pictures."

"Sammy looks so cute with curly hair," Zoe sobbed. "And J.T. is wearing the most adorable shorts!"

"Really? Let me see!" Katie said excitedly.

She edged Miriam over so she could get a better look at the screen.

The girls gave Katie a strange look.

"*You* like the Bayside Boys, Mr. Kane?" Suzanne asked.

Oops. Katie had almost forgotten that she was the principal. It must have seemed really weird to the girls that a grown man would be so interested in a pop group.

"No. I mean . . . well . . . um . . . gotta go!" Katie said quickly. She dashed out of the computer lab just as Kevin and Manny came running in.

"Mr. Kane, you're my favorite grown-up," Kevin said.

"Yeah. We're going to play Castle Craze now," Manny added. "It's so cool to be able to play computer games at school."

"Have a great time," she told the boys. "Remember, the best way to get to the fourth level is to capture the magic dragon."

"Wow!" Kevin exclaimed as Katie walked

away. "Mr. Kane knows how to play Castle Craze. How cool!"

"He's awesome," Manny agreed.

Katie smiled to herself. She didn't know when the magic wind was going to blow and turn her back into herself. But whenever that happened, Mr. Kane would be really happy. Katie had made him the most popular principal in the whole history of principals. The kids were so happy. Cherrydale Elementary School was the best school in the country. Maybe even in the whole *world*!

"*Owwww.*" Just then Katie heard George's voice. It sounded like he was in pain.

"Help me," he groaned. "Please."

# Chapter 7

Katie found George in the hall just outside the nurse's office. He was curled up in a ball, moaning.

"What's wrong?" Katie asked him.

"My stomach hurts," George answered. "I think I ate too much."

"How many pieces of chocolate cake did you have?"

George made a face when Katie mentioned the cake. "I don't know. Maybe thirteen or fourteen slices."

"George!" Katie shouted out. "That's an awful lot of cake."

"Uh-oh," George murmured. He grabbed

his stomach. His face looked a bit green.

Katie jumped out of the way. "Nurse Hanes," she called out. "George needs help."

"So do the rest of these kids," Nurse Hanes shouted from inside her office.

Katie walked into the nurse's office. There was a huge line of kids. Some had cuts and bruises. Others were sitting with ice packs on their knees and heads. "What's going on?" Katie asked.

"It's this 'no rules' thing," the nurse explained. "These kids were running in the halls and playing with all sorts of gym equipment. It was just a matter of time before someone got hurt. How am I going to take care of all these kids?"

Katie was about to answer, when a first-grader ran up and pulled on her pants. "Mr. Kane, hurry. There's gonna be a fight."

"A fight? Where?" Katie asked nervously.

"On the soccer field," the boy answered. "Jeremy's real mad. So's Ricky."

That wasn't good. It took a lot to get Jeremy angry.

Quickly, Katie grabbed a trash can and placed it near George's head. "If you feel sick, use that. I gotta go."

Katie dashed out of the school. She could hear the boys screaming as she ran toward the soccer field. Coach G. was blowing his whistle over and over. The boys weren't listening.

"What's going on?" Katie asked the gym teacher.

"It's the 'no rules' rule," Coach G. told her. "It's ruined the whole game."

Jeremy came running over. "Mr. Kane, can't we just have rules for soccer?" he begged.

"No way," Ricky Dobbs argued. He looked up at Katie. "You said 'no rules.' That means no rules anywhere."

"But you're using your hands in soccer," Jeremy said. "You can't do that unless you're the goalie. And you're not the goalie."

"There's no rule
saying I can't use my
hands. Not anymore,"
Ricky argued.

"You see what I
mean?" Coach G. asked
Katie. He handed her
his whistle. "Maybe
you should be the
referee for this game.
I can't figure out who's
winning in a game
with no rules."

Before Katie could answer, Suzanne came
running out to the field. "Mr. Kane, you'd better come to the computer lab. We were using
all the computers at once. Now none of the
computers are working—and the lights are
out all over the school.

"Oh no!" Katie moaned. She followed
Suzanne back into the dark school building.
As she opened the door, a stream of green

paint came flying toward her. It splattered all over Mr. Kane's white shirt. Katie looked down at the stain. The principal wasn't going to like this.

"What's going on in here?" Katie yelled.

"Paint fight," a sixth-grade girl named Justine told her. Justine ducked down to avoid being hit by a paint splatter. The red paint landed on Katie's bald head instead.

"How did this start?" Katie asked her.

"We took some supplies from the art room, and went to paint in the cafeteria," Justine explained. "Rachel's paint wound up on Dylan's jeans. So she painted his hair blue. After that, everyone got into it."

Katie sighed. This was not working out the way she'd thought it would. "Is the cafeteria a mess?" she asked.

"Not too bad," Justine answered. "There's a little paint on the walls. The mural's kind of messed up."

Oh, no. Not the mural Katie and her

friends had worked so hard on! Katie felt like she was about to cry. But she couldn't. Not here anyway. It wouldn't be good for the kids to see their principal cry.

Katie began running down the hall. She had to get to Mr. Kane's office right away. She could be alone there.

Whoosh! Katie slipped on a wet paint spot. She landed on her rear end and slid down the hall. A couple kids giggled.

Katie didn't feel like laughing at all.

# Chapter 8

Katie raced into Mr. Kane's office and slammed the door. She began to cry. It all was too much for a third-grade girl to handle. If only she were a real principal. Mr. Kane would know what to do. Katie was sure of it.

Just then, a small breeze floated through the office. The warm air tickled the back of Katie's neck. Katie reached over to grab the pile of papers on Mr. Kane's desk. She didn't want them to blow away.

But the papers weren't moving. Nothing in the office was.

Katie knew what that meant. The magic wind was back!

The wind began to grow stronger. It whipped around Katie so fast that it made a slight whistling sound as it blew. Katie was scared, but she didn't cry. Instead, she called out, "Please, please, please let me turn back into me! I just want to be Katie Carew again!"

Then the wind stopped suddenly. Katie looked around. She wasn't in Mr. Kane's office anymore. She was back in the cafeteria, where the whole mess had started.

Of course the cafeteria didn't look like it had back during recess. Now there were paint stains on the walls and pieces of cake ground into the floors.

Katie looked down at her clothes. Instead of Mr. Kane's white shirt and gray slacks, she was wearing her heart T-shirt and her skirt. She felt the top of her head. She had her hair. Good.

*Katie Carew was back.*

Just then, Suzanne came running up to her. "Where've you been, Katie?" she asked.

"I've been looking all over for you."

Katie wasn't sure what to say. Suzanne wouldn't believe the truth even if she told her. Who would?

"Oh, I've been around," Katie said finally.

"This has been some crazy day," Suzanne said. "Mr. Kane sure surprised everyone with this no rules thing."

Katie nodded. She had a feeling that no one was more surprised by it than Mr. Kane himself.

"I'm just glad today's over," Katie told her. She began to walk toward the front door of the school. It was time to go home.

"By the way, thanks for not telling Mr. Kane that the phone was mine," Suzanne said, as the two girls walked outside.

"It's okay," Katie assured her.

"Maybe we should ask for my phone back," Suzanne said as the girls left the school. "He said you could have it at the end of the day."

Katie looked over at the principal. He was

sitting on the front steps of the building. He looked like a mess. The parents he was talking to seemed really angry.

"I'd wait until tomorrow, Suzanne," Katie suggested.

"I don't understand how you let this happen," Katie heard Kevin's mother say.

"I'm not sure, either, Mrs. Camilleri," Mr. Kane admitted.

"Didn't you tell the students there were no rules in school?" Mrs. Chan asked.

Mr. Kane looked confused. "I don't know. I mean, I must have. But I don't really remember doing it."

"I think you need a rest, Mr. Kane," Mrs. Dobbs said in an angry voice. "A long rest."

Katie gulped. Mrs. Dobbs was the president of the school's PTA. If she was mad, Mr. Kane could be in real trouble.

# Chapter 9

The next morning, things on the playground seemed really weird. No one was playing. No one was laughing. No one was saying a word. Instead, the kids were standing in straight lines.

"What's going on?" Katie asked Manny as she took a place in line.

"Shhh," Manny whispered. "Do you want to get us in trouble?"

"Trouble?" Katie asked. "School hasn't even started yet."

"You. Come here!" A tall, skinny man with a small moustache called out.

"Who's that?" Katie asked Manny.

Before Manny could answer, the skinny man walked over to Katie. "Why are you talking?" he asked.

Katie didn't know what to say.

"We have a new rule here, Miss," the man said. "Students will line up quietly before school."

"Why?" Katie asked him.

"Because I said so," he replied. "And I'm your substitute principal, Mr. Ditherspoon. Everyone does what I want them to do."

Katie didn't say anything after that.

Mr. Ditherspoon looked at the students lined up before him. "There are going to be a lot of changes here," he told them. "For starters, there are new hair rules." Mr. Ditherspoon walked over to Caleb Connor, a sixth-grader who always wore big spikes in his hair. "You may not wear hair gel to school anymore. No one can. And girls with long hair must wear braids."

Katie didn't like the sound of that. Her hair was sometimes knotty and kind of curly. That made it really hard to braid.

"There will be no more T-shirts with words and pictures on them, either. Also, no more glitter—on your clothes or your faces. I want plain clothes and clean skin in my school."

Suzanne looked very upset. Everything she wore had glitter on it. With this new rule, she wouldn't have any school clothes at all.

"Okay, I want all of you to walk *silently* to class," Mr. Ditherspoon said as he opened the school doors. "Your teachers will fill you in on the rest of my new rules."

"You mean there are more?" George blurted out.

Mr. Ditherspoon glared at him. "I'll be watching you, Mr. Brennan," he growled.

Katie walked into her classroom, hung up her coat, put her homework on the pile, and sat at her desk. She pulled out a pencil and her notebook. But before she could begin her work, Mrs. Derkman pulled the pencil from her hand.

"This pencil point is too long," Mrs. Derkman said. She held up a ruler. "Mr. Ditherspoon doesn't want any pencil point to be more than one quarter inch long." She picked up Katie's notebook. "And from now on, every student must have plain black-and-white notebooks."

Katie looked down. She loved her note-book. On the cover, it had a picture of a puppy and a kitten in a basket. She didn't want a plain black-and-white notebook.

But that was the rule.

❄❄❄

At lunchtime, Katie slowly slid her tray along the line. When it was her turn, she smiled at Lucille the Lunch Lady. "I'll have the peas, the mashed potatoes, a glass of milk, and some rice pudding."

Lucille shook her head. "Sorry. You can't have dessert unless you eat the whole meal. And today we have hamburgers."

"But I don't eat meat," Katie told her.

"Then you don't eat pudding, either," Lucille told her. "That's Mr. Ditherspoon's rule."

Katie sighed. "Just the peas, the potatoes, and the milk, then." She took her tray and walked toward her class's table.

"Move over," she whispered to Jeremy. Katie wasn't sure if they were still allowed to talk at lunch. Nobody else seemed to be saying anything.

Jeremy slid his chair over and made room

for Katie. He took his fork and began to mush his peas together with his mashed potatoes.

Just then, Mr. Ditherspoon appeared at his side. "What are you doing with those peas?" he asked.

"Mixing them with my potatoes," Jeremy explained.

"You can't do that."

Jeremy pushed his glasses up on his nose nervously. "But I always eat them that way," he said quietly.

Mr. Ditherspoon glared at Jeremy. "There's only one way to eat at this school. And that's my way. If you want that dessert, you have to eat the hamburger, then the peas, then the mashed potatoes. There will be no mixing foods at my school!"

"Yes, sir," Jeremy mumbled quietly. He picked up his burger and took a bite.

"And make sure you chew each bite twenty-three times . . . exactly," Mr. Ditherspoon told him.

Jeremy chewed.

Katie looked around at her friends' sad faces. This was all her fault. If she hadn't gotten rid of all the rules at school, Mr. Kane would still be the principal. Things were really horrible now. And there didn't seem to be anything she could do about it.

# Chapter 10

When Katie got home, she ran right up to her room and slammed the door. She was in a terrible mood. This had been the worst day ever. Katie's chocolate-and-white cocker spaniel, Pepper, scratched at her door. But Katie didn't open it. She didn't want to see anyone. Not even Pepper.

The phone rang downstairs. "Katie, it's for you," her mom called out.

Katie frowned. She really didn't feel like talking to any of her friends. "Who is it?" she asked.

"Suzanne," her mother answered. "She says it's important."

Katie ran downstairs and took the phone from her mother. "What?" she asked in a grumpy voice.

"Hello to you, too," Suzanne teased.

"I'm sorry," Katie apologized. "I'm just in a bad mood. Today was awful."

"Oh, yeah!" Suzanne agreed. "And it's going to get worse."

"What do you mean?"

"We might have Mr. Ditherspoon as our principal forever," Suzanne said.

"I thought he was just a substitute," Katie told her.

"He is," Suzanne agreed. "But my mom says the PTA is thinking about recommending him as our new principal."

"What about Mr. Kane?"

"There's going to be a big school board meeting on Friday. They might fire Mr. Kane," Suzanne told Katie.

"We have to stop them!" Katie exclaimed.

"Forget it, Katie. This is the *school board*.

They're not going to listen to kids," Suzanne told her.

"I'm not so sure about that. Remember, that's what you said when Mr. Kane fired Lucille," Katie reminded her. "But we got her job back for her."

It was true. Mr. Kane had fired the lunch lady after she'd gotten into a foodfight with some of the kids. Of course, it had actually been *Katie* who had gotten into the foodfight, but Mr. Kane didn't know that. He didn't know about the magic wind. The kids had saved Lucille's job by refusing to eat the cafeteria food until Mr. Kane hired her back.

"That's true," Suzanne said. "But I have no idea how we can get Mr. Kane back. Do you?"

Katie thought about it for a minute. Then she smiled. "I think I do. Will you help me?"

"Sure," Suzanne agreed. "I'll do anything to be allowed to wear glitter again!"

# Chapter 11

As Katie walked into the school board meeting, her stomach was very jumpy. Some people might say she had butterflies in her tummy. But Katie thought they felt more like elephants. A whole herd of elephants . . . stampeding!

"Are you scared?" Jeremy whispered to Katie as they took their seats.

"Are you?" Katie asked.

Jeremy nodded. "I've never spoken in front of this many grown-ups before."

Katie looked over to where Suzanne was sitting with her parents. Even *she* looked nervous.

The meeting seemed to drag on forever. Lots and lots of grown-ups gave long speeches about how awful Mr. Kane's no-rules day was.

Mr. Kane didn't say anything. He just sat in the front of the room, looking very confused. Every now and then he wiped a bead of sweat from his forehead.

"Does anyone else have anything to say before we vote?" the head of the school board, Mr. Rosen, asked finally.

Katie raised her hand shyly.

"Yes?" Mr. Rosen pointed toward Katie.

Katie gulped. Everyone was staring at her. It was really scary. But Katie knew she had to say something. She had to save Mr. Kane.

Katie walked up to the front of the room. "My name is Katie Carew," she said. "I'm in class 3A, and I like Mr. Kane."

"That's very nice, Katie," Mr. Rosen said. "But, as grown-ups, we have to make sure school is a place where you can learn."

"But we learned a lot that day," Katie said.

"What could you possibly have learned on
a no-rules day?" Mr. Rosen asked.

"We learned that rules are really important." Katie stopped and thought about Mr.
Ditherspoon's pencil point rule. "Well, at
least *most* rules," she added.

"Really?" Mr. Rosen said with surprise.

Katie nodded. "We even came up with some rules of our own." She turned toward Jeremy and Suzanne. They stood up, too.

"I think it's important to do your homework," Katie began. "And there shouldn't be any fighting in school, either."

"Kids should be able to wear what they want," Suzanne continued. "But no one should be allowed to make fun of someone else's outfit."

"Or their drawings," Katie added. "You shouldn't make fun of anyone for any reason."

"There have to be rules in sports," Jeremy said. "And I think new kids should be paired up with a buddy on their first day of school. Then they could have a friend right away."

"We should have a student government at school," Katie told the school board. "I think kids would follow rules more easily if they got to make some of them."

Katie looked over at Mr. Kane. He didn't

seem so nervous anymore. He seemed proud. The principal stood up and began to clap. Soon most of the parents in the room were on their feet and clapping, too.

Mr. Rosen smiled at the kids. "Well, I guess you did learn something that day," he began.

"Mr. Kane is very smart," Katie told him.

"Yes, he is." Mr. Rosen agreed. He turned toward Mr. Kane. "There's no way we could possibly fire you now."

"Thank you," Mr. Kane said.

"But I do have one question," Mr. Rosen continued. "Why didn't you tell anyone about your plan?"

Mr. Kane gulped. He fiddled with his tie. He looked at his shoes. What could he say? He had no idea what had happened that day.

"Mr. Kane couldn't have told anyone," Katie quickly said. "It *had* to be a surprise. Otherwise, we never would have learned the lesson ourselves."

Everyone started clapping again.

"Good one, Katie," Suzanne whispered. "Grown-ups love when you say stuff like that."

# Chapter 12

The meeting didn't last much longer. When it was over, Mr. Kane walked over to Katie, Suzanne, and Jeremy.

"I don't how to thank you kids," he said. "I'm not quite sure what happened this week. But I am glad it turned out this way. You had some great ideas."

Katie smiled. She thought so, too.

"So who wants ice cream?" Mr. Kane asked. "My treat!"

Talk about a great idea!

As Katie walked outside with her friends and her parents, she felt a breeze hit the back of her neck. Her smile turned to a frown. This

was awful. She didn't want to turn into anyone else. She just wanted to stay Katie
Carew—and have a big rocky road ice cream
cone.

"Whoa, it's getting cold!" Suzanne zipped
the front of her sparkly black jacket. "Feel
that wind."

Katie smiled brightly. It wasn't the magic
wind after all. It was just a plain, old wind.
One that could blow on anyone.

"I think it feels wonderful!" she said.

# Chapter 13

**Class 3A's Favorite Playground Games!**

George is the king of Four Square. Suzanne loves to play Statue Tag. Jeremy's favorite game is soccer, but he's always ready to play Poison. Now you and your friends can play these games too. Here's how.

**Four Square** (a game for four players)

You will need: Chalk, a kickball

You can draw a four square court on any playground. Draw a large square, sixteen feet wide by sixteen feet long. Now divide it into four smaller squares of equal size. The smaller squares should be four feet wide by four feet long. (You can get a grown-up to help you with this part.)

One player stands in each square. One square is called the king. The other squares are called the queen, the prince, and the princess. The king is the highest-ranking square. The princess is the lowest-ranking square.

To start the game, the king serves the ball by bouncing it in his square and then hitting it to any of the other players. That player has to let the ball bounce, and then hit it to any other player. Then that player has to hit the ball to another player.

Keep going until one of these things happens:

*A player hits the ball before it bounces in her square.

*A player does not hit the ball.

*A player hits the ball out of bounds. (The ball has to land in someone's square.)

If anything like that happens, the player

who made the mistake has to move to the princess square. The other players move up to fill the empty squares.

At the end of recess, the player in the king's box is the winner.

**Statue Tag** (a game for ten or more players)

You will need: chalk

Use the chalk to make a starting line. Then choose one player to be *it*. *It* must stand about fifty feet away from the line with her back to the other players.

*It* counts to ten. While she's counting, the other players run or walk toward her. As soon as it reaches ten, she turns around.

That's when all the other players stand still like statues. Anyone caught moving (even a little, teensy bit) has to go back to the starting line.

Then *it* turns around and begins to count to ten again.

As soon as any player is close enough to tag *it*, he should. Just be sure her back is turned, because if she sees you moving, you have to go back to the starting line.

The first player to tag *it*, becomes the new *it*.

**Poison** (a game for five or more players)
You will need: a pot

The players all join hands, making a circle around the pot. One player is chosen to be the leader. He tries to push or pull the other players so that one of them knocks a foot against the pot.

As soon as any player touches the pot, he becomes poison. All the other players have to run away from him. The player who is poison has to try and catch one of the other players. That person becomes the new leader, and the game begins again.